A note from the author

Pepper Zhang, Artist Extraordinaire! is a book made possible because of you.

I'm just a father who wanted to write a book for his daughters to show them that a little Asian girl is deserving of the spotlight in a children's book.

Little did I know that Pepper Zhang would resonate with so many parents and children around the world.

Thank you for allowing me the privilege to share Pepper's story.

Jerry Zhang

To my girls

A special thank you to Bryan Cheah

Printed in China by Four Color Print Group, Louisville, Kentucky.
First Edition
ISBN 978-0-9990877-0-1
ISBN 978-0-9990877-3-2 (ebook)

Pepper Zhang

Artist Extraordinaire!

Written by Jerry Zhang

Illustrated by Trisha Hautéa

Little Ning Books

It all began with a paint set, an easel ...

and a tantrum.

You see, Pepper Zhang is a girl of many strong emotions,

and on the night of her third birthday, she summoned her strongest emotions and directed them all toward a single goal:

NOT
GOING
TO
BED!

PEPPER'S EMOTIONS CREATED A **LOUD** AND **BOOMING** RACKET THAT RUMBLED DOWN THE HALL LIKE rolling thunder!

All seemed hopeless as **Pepper**'s tantrum reached a boiling point!

But then, suddenly,

it all stopped -

because out of the corner of her eye, Pepper spotted the one
birthday gift she hadn't played with that day - a paint set and
easel from Nai Nai and Ye Ye.

And just like that, Pepper's tantrum was over.

Everyone rushed out of her room as she began to paint feverishly!

Though her family didn't know it at the time, on that fateful night, amidst all the fury, anger, and frustration ...

AN ARTI

T WAS BORN!

With a few strokes of the paint brush, Pepper painted
her first work of art

which she fittingly titled, *Red Dino Destroys Bedtime!*

(artist's interpretation)

After that night,

Pepper kept painting

and painting

and painting

and had fewer and fewer tantrums, which delighted her parents!

Over time, Pepper's room slowly transformed ...

into her very own private art gallery
that showcased all of her work.

Eventually, news about Pepper's art began to spread -

and people from all
over the world came
to see and admire her
art work!

Her fans all proclaimed her:

"PEPPER ZHANG, ARTIST EXTRAORDINAIRE!"

- a nickname she proudly embraced!

Within a short time, her fame soared to great heights

along with her art!

PEPPER WAS UNSTOPPABLE!

But then a peculiar thing happened...

The more famous Pepper became, the larger her head

grew

and grew

and grew!

Unfortunately, Pepper's new big head caused big problems for her,

like making it impossible to paint!

Which didn't make her
feel like an artist, or very
extraordinary at all.

So despite all the fame, glory, and acclaim,

Pepper decided to close her gallery and take a break from being "Pepper Zhang, Artist Extraordinaire!,"

focus on being "Pepper Zhang,
Amazing Daughter and Big Sister."

Eventually, Pepper's head shrunk back to its normal size, and she returned to being a regular three-year-old, doing regular three-year-old things.

But not to worry!

This is definitely not the
last you've heard of

"Pepper Zhang,
Artist Extraordinaire!"